Myths of
The Native
AMERICANS

Anita Dalal

RSVP

RAINTREE
STECK-VAUGHN
PUBLISHERS

A Steck-Vaughn Company

Steck-Vaughn Company

First published 2001 by Raintree Steck-Vaughn Publishers, an imprint of Steck-Vaughn Company.

© 2002 Brown Partworks Limited

Library of Congress Cataloging-in-Publication Data

Dalal, Anita.
    Myths of native Americans / Anita Dalal.
        p. cm. -- (Mythic world)
    Includes bibliographical references and index.
    ISBN 0-7398-3190-9
        1. Aztec mythology--United States--Juvenile literature. 2. Indian mythology--Canada--Juvenile literature. 3. Indians of North America--Juvenile literature. [1. Indians of North America--Folklore. 2. Indians of North America--Religion. 3. Folklore--North America.] I. Title. II. Series.

    E98.R3 D135 2001
    398.2'089'97--dc21

                                                  2001019817

Printed and bound in the United States
1 2 3 4 5 6 7 8 9 IP 05 04 03 02 01

Series Consultant: C. Scott Littleton, Professor of Anthropology,
Occidental College, Los Angeles
Volume Author: Anita Dalal

for Brown Partworks
Project Editor: Lee Stacy
Designer: Sarah Williams
Picture Researcher: Helen Simm
Indexer: Kay Ollerenshaw
Managing Editor: Tim Cooke
Design Manager: Lynne Ross
Production Manager: Matt Weyland

for Raintree Steck-Vaughn
Project Editor: Sean Dolan
Production Manager: Richard Johnson

Picture credits

Cover: Acoma: Corbis/Adam Woolfitt; Iroquois mask: Peter Newark's American Pictures

Ancient Art & Architecture Collection: B. Norman 9b; **The Art Archive:** 9t; **Bruce Coleman Collection:** 19, Johnny Johnson 35; **Corbis:** 12, Tom Bean 40, Bettmann 25t, Jonathan Blair 11, W. Perry Conway 39, Peter Hardholt 36, Neil Rabinowitz 32; **Mary Evans Picture Library:** 25b; **Brown Partworks Ltd:** National Archives 41t; **NHPA:** Stephen Krasemann 27, 28; **North Wind Pictures:** 7; **Peter Newark's American Pictures:** 5, 8, 13, 16, 17b, 17t, 20, 23, 29b, 37t, 45b, 45t; **Seattle Art Museum:** Paul Macapia 31; **Still Pictures:** J.J. Alcalay 44, B&C Alexander 29t, Hubert Klein 15, Robert Schoen 37b; **Werner Forman Archive:** 21b, 33; **Field Museum of Natural History Chicago:** 21t, 41b; **Schindler Collection New York:** 24: White buffalo page 43 courtesy of **Spiritual Endeavours,** www.spiritualendeavours.org.

Contents

General Introduction

MYTHS ARE THE MIRRORS of humanity. They reflect the inner soul of a culture and try to give profound answers in a seemingly mysterious world. In other words, myths give the relevant culture an understanding of its place in the world and the universe in general. Found in all civilizations, myths sometimes combine fact and fiction and other times are complete fantasy. Regardless of their creative origin, myths are always dramatic.

Every culture has its own myths, yet globally there are common themes and symbols, even across civilizations that had no contact with or awareness of each other. Some of the most common types include those that deal with the creation of the world, the cosmos, or a particular site, like a large mountain or lake. Other myths deal with the origin of humans, or a specific people or civilization, or the heroes or gods who either made the world inhabitable or gave humans something essential, such as the ancient Greek Titan Prometheus, who gave fire, or the Ojibwa hero Wunzh, who was given divine instructions on cultivating corn. There are also myths about the end of the world, death and the afterlife, and the renewal or change of seasons.

The origin of evil and death are also common themes. Examples of such myths are the Biblical Eve eating the forbidden fruit or the ancient Greek story of Pandora opening the sealed box.

Additionally there are flood myths, myths about the sun and the moon, and myths of a peaceful, beautiful place of reward, such as heaven or Elysium, or of punishment, such as hell or Tartarus. Myths also teach important human values, such as courage. In all cases, myths show that the gods and their deeds are outside of ordinary human life and yet essential to it.

In this volume some of the most important Native American myths are presented. Following each myth is an explanation of how the myth was either reflected in or linked to the real life of the particular Native American tribe or tribal group. There is also a glossary at the end of the volume to help identify the major mythological and historical characters, as well as explain many cultural terms.

NATIVE AMERICAN MYTHOLOGY

When Christopher Columbus first set foot on the Caribbean island of San Salvador in 1492, the vast North American continent was populated by several million people. For the most part these peoples lived in small communities, many of which were linked together by a similar or common language and customs, forming large tribes. Each tribe — or even individual community — had its own body of myths that related directly to the group's way of life in its native environment. Depending on

Above: *This painting by George Catlin from about 1850 shows a Crow tepee decorated with scenes of war and buffalo hunting. Native Americans had many myths about buffalo and other animals important to their lives.*

where and how the tribe lived, the myths included, among other things, explanations of the existence of water, corn, fish, and buffalo — the relevant essentials for survival — as well as the origin of the earth and the tribe itself.

The environment was at the heart of Native American life, and it was believed that the spirit world originated and controlled all nature. As in many cultures around the world, Native American myths were reflected in rituals. Often celebrated using a combination of face- and body-painting, chanting and singing, dancing, and playing music, usually on drums and rattles, rituals reenacted scenes from myths, as dancers

portrayed characters from these sacred stories. Such rituals were intended to maintain the harmony between people and the spirit beings.

Shamans, or medicine men, were also responsible for maintaining a good relationship between the tribe and the spirit world. More than healers, shamans, such as Sitting Bull of the Sioux, could command enormous influence in the community and were accorded a great deal of respect. They were highly perceptive individuals who had to go through a long period of physically difficult and emotionally intense training before they could be expected to fully understand and communicate with the supernatural.

The Dueling Brothers

The Iroquois, who originated this myth, were one of the largest tribes in the vast Eastern Woodlands region, ranging from the Great Lakes and the Mississippi River to the Atlantic seaboard.

AT THE BEGINNING OF TIME, high up in the sky, lived the Great Chief, his wife, and the celestial people. There was a thin, hard crust at the bottom of their sky village and none of the celestial people knew what lay beneath. In the center of the sky village grew a huge tree, full of fruits and flowers, that fed the celestial people. On the top of the huge tree was a large flower that gave out light, brightening up their world.

One day, the Great Chief's wife told her husband that she was pregnant. He immediately grew angry and pulled up the huge tree, exposing a wide, deep hole. He pushed his wife into it.

The hole led through the clouds and as the Chief's wife was falling, two ducks living on the water-covered world below spread their wings, breaking her fall. The ducks brought the woman to their chief, the Great Turtle, who at once summoned an assembly of the animals.

The Great Turtle knew that some dirt from the roots of the celestial tree must have fallen down with the woman. He commanded all the animals to find where the dirt had sunk and bring it to him. All the animals looked high and low, searching in every nook and cranny beneath the watery surface. But out of all the animals, only the little toad managed to find some celestial dirt.

He spread it onto the Great Turtle's shell. The dirt was full of magic and soon it had grown to the size of an island where the Great Chief's wife could live.

Months later she gave birth to a daughter. For many years the Great Chief's wife lived happily with her beautiful daughter on the island. Then one day the daughter, out walking on her own, got pregnant by the wind. She gave birth to twins. The older one emerged gentle and kind, but the younger one was evil and killed his young mother as she gave birth to him.

Saddened at the death of her daughter, the Great Chief's wife raised the boys. The older one, named Tsentsa, worked hard creating fruit trees and pretty bushes. But the younger boy, Taweskare, was determined to destroy all the good works of his older brother and made the fruit small and covered the bushes in thorns. When Tsentsa made fish smooth, Taweskare covered them in sharp scales. Taweskare also bewitched many of the animals, and he made the snakes poisonous. He made wintertime cold and snowy, too.

Above: *This illustration shows how Native Americans harvested corn. The traditional method for harvesting corn involved the whole community and included removing the husk from the stalk, then gathering the husks in baskets.*

After years of conflict the two brothers finally fought each other. Tsentsa defeated his evil brother, and Taweskare was forced to travel west. There his anger created many volcanoes that still belch smoke, ooze rivers of hot mud, and cause the earth to tremble. Today his anger can be seen and felt through volcanoes. Tsentsa stayed in the east and became the father of the Iroquois, teaching them how to farm and make fire, among many other good things.

Adapting for Survival

North America is a land and climate of extremes, and each tribe faced its own set of struggles with nature to survive. The obstacles ranged from ice to drought, bears to rattlesnakes.

Tsentsa, the hero of the Iroquois (see page 6) and one of the tribe's principal gods, was believed to have taught the tribespeople how to survive. Explaining that nature can provide food and other material for survival, if one knows how and when to look for it, is common in Native American myths.

Native America can be divided into 10 culture areas, each with its own unique environment. These are the Arctic, Subarctic, Northwest Coast, California, Basin, Plateau, Southwest, Great Plains, Southeast, and Eastern Woodlands. Of these the Eastern Woodlands, Plains, Southwest, and Arctic are good examples of environmental extremes.

LEARNING FROM THE PAST

Various survival techniques were passed down to Native Americans from ancient peoples such as the Adena and Mississippians, who built large cities with ceremonial mounds in the South, and the Anasazi and Hohokam, who learned how to farm in the dry Southwest. These peoples thrived hundreds of years before tribes such as the Iroquois.

The Iroquois were actually a union of six tribes, also known as the Iroquois Confederacy, who lived in the vast Eastern Woodlands. These tribes were the Mohawk, Oneida, Onondaga, Cayuga, Seneca, and Tuscarora. Their union, or league, was formed between 1570 and 1600, long before European settlers came to dominate this enormous region.

One reason why the union worked well together was that the individual tribes spoke a similar language and

Above: *Using a forked spear, this Ojibwa man, photographed in 1900, fishes in the traditional manner of the Subarctic and Eastern Woodlands tribes.*

Left: *This realistic scene of an Osage man catching a wild horse was painted by the 19th-century artist George Catlin.*

shared a common way of life. They lived in small enclosed villages made up of longhouses and farmed and hunted in the same way. The Iroquois, like most other major Eastern Woodlands tribes, hunted deer and moose, fished in rivers and lakes, and planted crops that included corn, beans, and squashes.

In contrast to the Woodlands tribes, the Plains tribes, like the Sioux, had no fixed home but moved across the wide, open, flat spaces in pursuit of buffalo herds. Their tepees, made of lightweight poles and buffalo hides, were ideally suited for traveling great distances.

Plains tribes lived mostly off of buffalo, deer, and wild plants. During the mid-17th century they began to experience a dramatic change to their life style. The horse arrived on the Plains, and Native Americans quickly learned to ride the fast animals and use them for hunting, among other things.

The tribes of the Southwest region were primarily farmers, although they also hunted small game such as rabbit. Southwestern tribes, such as the Pueblo, Hopi, and Navajo, developed a network of irrigation systems that proved successful for raising crops such as corn, beans, and squashes. The tribes of this region lived in permanent structures — called pueblos — made of adobe, sometimes embedded in a giant rockface or atop a mountain for protection against enemy tribes.

Much farther north, in the Arctic region, peoples such as the Inuit learned to find food in a landscape frozen for much of the year. The Inuit arrived in North America nearly 30,000 years after the first group of nomads crossed the Bering Strait into Alaska around 33,000 B.C. The Inuit relied on fishing and hunting large marine mammals such as whales, seals, and walruses. Harpooning a whale was dangerous, but such prey provided enough meat to feed several families for a long time.

Below: *Although this pueblo in Taos, New Mexico, is centuries old, the doors and windows are relatively recent additions. In more hostile times in the past, the only openings were in the roofs, making it hard for enemies to get in.*

The Hopi in the Desert

The Hopi created this myth to try to explain the origin and diversity of tribes and languages in the Southwest. This myth is similar to certain myths told by other tribes of the region.

A VERY LONG TIME AGO the ancient people, who were the forefathers of all the tribes, lived underground, in a perfect paradise where everybody was happy and all their needs were satisfied. After a while the ancient people began to take their perfect life for granted. They became lazy and greedy, demanding things from the underworld that they did not actually need.

As punishment for the ancient people's complacency and greed, the spirits of the underworld made the water in all the ponds, lakes, and rivers rise. Soon all the houses and villages were flooded and everybody feared they would drown. Only Spider Woman and Mockingbird felt sorry for the ancient people. Together they decided to help them escape.

Spider Woman showed the ancient people to a giant reed that led to two types of large pine tree. The tops of the trees were joined to a huge sunflower that rose to a tunnel high above the rising water. Mockingbird sat at the entrance of the tunnel, assigning a tribe and a language to each person as they entered. To one person he sang, "You will belong to the Hopi tribe and speak their language," to another, "You are now an Apache and will speak their tongue," or "You will be one of the Navajo and talk the way they talk."

There were so many ancient people that Mockingbird sat singing his assignments for several long days. Eventually he grew too tired to sing, leaving many people trapped in the underworld without a tribe or language. But all those who had been given a tribe and a language climbed through the tunnel to the earth's surface.

The tunnel opened onto the desert. But in those days the earth was still covered in darkness, so the ancient people decided to set off in search of sunlight. They agreed that each tribe should travel in different directions. The so-called White People, who were a separate group of Hopi, went east while the other tribes started off on foot in all directions. Only the remaining Hopi and the other Pueblo peoples stayed in the desert where they had come out of the ground.

The tribes had agreed that the first group to find the sun would send a signal to all the other tribes by causing a shower of stars to shoot across the sky. Upon seeing the shooting stars all the other tribes were to stop where they were and make that place their home forever.

Above: *Not far from the place where the Hopi supposedly emerged from the underworld, this meteor shower filled the sky in December 1985. Perhaps it was just such a brilliant nighttime display described in the ancient myth.*

The White People were very impatient and did not want to travel on foot. So their women rubbed flakes of skin from their bodies, which they then molded into fast horses. With the help of the horses they raced to the east, where the sun rises, and so became the first tribe to see it.

As promised, the White People sent a great shower of bright stars racing across the sky, and when the other tribes saw the shooting stars they stopped traveling and settled. This is why the Hopi and Pueblo peoples, who had not moved, ended up living in the desert.

The Evolution of Native American Languages

When Christopher Columbus claimed the so-called New World for Spain in 1492, there were millions of people speaking hundreds of languages and dialects in North America.

Although the Hopi myth (see page 10) does not specify how many languages Mockingbird assigned to the different Native American peoples, anthropologists believe that before the arrival of European settlers North America (north of Mexico) was home to about 240 different tribes or peoples, with as many as 500 distinct languages. All this diversity was found in a population of less than 10 million.

The 500 different languages can then be divided further into at least 2,000 separate dialects. With so many different tongues among a relatively small population, communication was often difficult between neighboring tribes and even between different bands — small camps, villages, or communities — within the same tribe.

The reason for the lack of a single Native American language was the geographical isolation of tribes and bands. Often bands lived in their own close-knit world with their own mythology and religion. These beliefs stemmed from their history and local surroundings. Their language was also influenced by their environment. For example the Hopi of the dry Southwest had numerous terms for drought.

Sometimes the names commonly used for tribes today were actually

Below: *By 1939, when this photo was taken, most Native American children spoke only English in the schools they shared with white children.*

tribal names given to them by their enemies. The name "Sioux" is an Ojibwa word for snake and literally means "enemy." Other tribal names were made up by the European missionaries, traders, and explorers.

Also, as trade increased between tribes, so did the mixture and expansion of languages. For example, the Sioux word "tepee" entered the vocabulary of both other Native Americans and European settlers. In addition, many place-names are originally tribal words, such as Chicago ("place of onions").

SPREADING LANGUAGES

Over the centuries, as tribes moved around North America, their language went with them. It was possible for two tribes who spoke a related language to end up thousands of miles away from each other. For example, the Navajo and the Apache tribes of the Southwest speak Athapascan languages, which are related to those of the peoples of the Subarctic. The other major tribal language groups include Algonquian, Caddoan, Iroquoian, Muskogean, and Siouan.

Despite so many different languages and dialects, by the early 20th century the dominance of white settlers had forced most North American Indian languages into virtual extinction. For example, today only a handful of tribespeople are left who speak Osage. Some tribal languages are still vibrant, however. For example, there are over 100,000 tribespeople on reservations who speak Navajo.

Below: Sequoya, the creator of the Cherokee alphabet, was a great linguist. In addition to his native tongue, he spoke English, French, and Spanish.

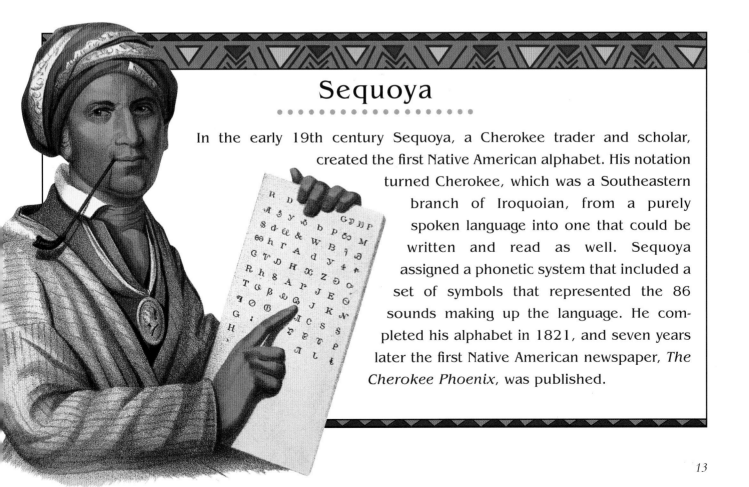

Sequoya

In the early 19th century Sequoya, a Cherokee trader and scholar, created the first Native American alphabet. His notation turned Cherokee, which was a Southeastern branch of Iroquoian, from a purely spoken language into one that could be written and read as well. Sequoya assigned a phonetic system that included a set of symbols that represented the 86 sounds making up the language. He completed his alphabet in 1821, and seven years later the first Native American newspaper, *The Cherokee Phoenix*, was published.

Old Man Coyote Creates Nature

The Crow, who lived in modern-day Wyoming and Montana, believed that before the great animal spirits made the world, water covered everything. Many tribes had similar beliefs.

A LONG TIME AGO the earth was completely covered with water. Old Man Coyote, who lived on his own, was bored and wanted someone to talk to. One day, when he was feeling lonely, he met two ducks.

"Is there nothing here but water?" he asked them. The ducks shrugged their shoulders and said they didn't know. He suggested that one of them dive down to see what they could find. The younger duck volunteered and dove down deep, staying there for a very long time.

When he surfaced the duck was carrying a little root and some mud. Old Man Coyote blew on the mud, and it began to grow and spread everywhere. He then took the root and planted it in the ground. Soon plants and trees grew, full of flowers and food to eat. Then he made rivers, ponds, and springs for fresh drinking water.

He was pleased with his work but felt something was missing. He had no other companions. To remedy this he took some mud and created people, but the ducks were unhappy because they too wanted companions. Coyote made more ducks and everybody was happy. Then they realized they needed some other types of animals, so he made

buffalo, deer, elk, antelopes, and bears. Now there were lots of animals and people, but they were bored because they had nothing to do.

To liven up things Coyote made a bird who danced at dawn. The animals watched the dancing bird, and soon they too were dancing. Only the bears refused to dance; they wanted a dance just for them. Old Man Coyote made a drum so the animals could have music while they danced. Still the bears grumbled, so Old Man Coyote punished them, commanding, "You will sleep half the year and live in a den all alone and eat rotten food." From that time on, that is how bears have lived.

The people and animals lived together in harmony, but the people had very little food. Nor did they have tools, tepees, or fire with which to cook or warm themselves. Old Man Coyote made a fire with lightning, and the people were pleased because they could cook and keep warm.

But Old Man Coyote was not yet finished. Realizing that they needed to kill animals for food, he made weapons for the people. He also decided to separate them into tribes that spoke different languages. This led to battles between the tribes, and the people used the weapons to kill each other.

Left: *Many Native American myths featured the coyote, as in Old Man Coyote, or its close cousin the wolf. Found throughout North America west of the Appalachian Mountains, the coyote was highly respected for its cunning by most western tribes.*

Native American Ceremonies

Life-changing events, such as birth, death, and war, were ritually celebrated by Native Americans, as were issues of survival, such as the harvest and the hunt.

Above: *During most tribal ceremonies masks, such as this Iroquoian mask, were worn by various members of the tribe, ranging from warriors to shamans. Usually these ritual performers would be dancing, often to drumbeats.*

Throughout Native America spirits often took the form of animals, and for the Crow tribe Old Man Coyote, who among other things invented dancing, was a very important spirit. The reason animals were commonly used in myths was that tribes across North America depended solely on wildlife and nature for their survival.

To show their appreciation to nature and the spirits, whom they believed controlled all aspects of life, many Native Americans often held long and elaborate rituals involving the local community and sometimes the whole tribe. The rituals were held to influence and celebrate changes in an individual's life, such as birth, marriage, and death, and the concerns of the community, such as a good harvest, a successful hunt, and victory in battle.

During public ceremonies principal performers would paint their faces or bodies and spend hours and sometimes days dancing, singing, and chanting. The music that accompanied many of these rituals was usually played on drums, rattles, and flutes.

THE SUN DANCE

Dance was extremely important for Native Americans and held deep religious significance. Every movement had a specific meaning. One of the best examples of the value tribes gave to dance was the Sun Dance ceremony. Adopted by many Plains tribes in the 19th century, the Sun Dance was much more than just a dance. It was an important annual ritual, usually held in early summer, where tribal members would renew their spiritual beliefs.

The ceremony lasted several days, and the whole tribe would, among other things, gather to dance, feast, arrange marriages, and hunt buffalo.

Left: *The Mandan buffalo dance, as seen in this painting by artist Karl Bodmer from 1833–1834, was an important ceremony of this Plains tribe.*

At the start of the Sun Dance a high pole was erected in the center of a lodge or open area, around which several dancers would perform. The pole symbolized the tribe's connection with nature and paid respect to all growing things.

In some instances, a few dancers would attach themselves to the pole with thongs tied to skewers inserted through the skin on their chests. Throughout the festival these dancers fasted and danced to the sound of a drumbeat, gradually pulling themselves away from the pole until the skewers were torn from their flesh. The people who danced in this way did so not to prove how tough or brave they were but because they were seeking spiritual energy and insight.

FUNERAL RITES

Other ceremonies involved rituals surrounding death. Most tribes believed that the dead could affect the world of the living, and so Native American funerals were meant to make sure that the spirits of the dead were kept happy. In the Eastern Woodlands the Iroquois held an annual celebration known as the Feast of the Dead. Although it was specifically for those who had died during the previous year, all the spirits of dead people were invited so that they would know that they were still remembered and respected.

Below: *In the mid-1830s, the artist George Catlin made this painting of a Mandan ritual that was similar to the Sun Dance.*

Coyote and the Dead

In many Native American myths the coyote is a cunning trickster. This tale comes from the Wishram, a Chinook Indian group from the Chinook Mountains of the Pacific Northwest.

WHEN THE TRICKSTER Coyote's sister died he grew very sad. Coyote's friend Eagle was also sad because he had lost his wife. Together Coyote and Eagle decided to travel to the land of the spirits where the dead dwelled. Once there they would bring back the spirits of their loved ones.

Well into their journey they came to a large body of water where they waited until dark. Coyote began to sing, and before long four spirit men appeared and ferried them across the water to the land of the dead.

There they entered a great tule-mat lodge where the spirits of the dead were dancing and singing under the light of the moon, which was inside the lodge. The spirits were beautifully dressed and their bodies and faces painted. The master of the lodge was Frog, who stood next to the moon.

Early in the morning the spirits left the lodge for their day of sleep. Coyote seized the moment and killed Frog, putting on his skin. That night the spirits returned to dance and sing. Coyote, in Frog's skin, waited until the dancing and singing were in full swing and then swallowed the moon.

In the darkness, Eagle caught the spirits and put them into Coyote's basket. The cunning pair shut the lid tightly, then started back to the land of the living. Coyote carried the basket and Eagle flew overhead, guiding their way. From inside the basket they could hear noises. The spirits were asking to be let out.

Finally the basket got too heavy for Coyote. "Let's let them out," he said, thinking the spirits were so far from the land of the dead that they could not return. So he put down the basket and opened the lid. The spirits, moving as fast as the wind, flew out of the box and headed straight for the land of the dead.

At first Eagle was angry with Coyote. Then he said, "It is now fall. The leaves are falling just like the animals die. Let's wait till the spring when everything is new and try to catch them again." But Coyote was tired and had decided that the spirits should stay in the land of the dead forever.

Coyote then made a law that a living thing that died could not come to life again. But if he had not opened the basket and let the spirits out, then the dead would come to life again every spring, just as grass, flowers, and trees do.

Above: *Coyotes often hunt alone, and many people view the animals as being self-reliant yet cunning and untrustworthy. These are the attributes that made Native Americans think of them as mythological tricksters.*

Tricksters and Shamans

The mysteries of life were celebrated by all Native Americans and specifically by each community's shaman. The shaman was the link between the natural world and the spirit world.

Left: *A Huron hunter blows smoke into the mouth of a bear he has killed. This was a way for him to thank the bear and make peace with its spirit.*

Each Native American tribe had its own animal trickster, which was often a complex and unpredictable character with the traits of its species greatly exaggerated. Coyote was the chief trickster for the Wishram and other tribes. He was cunning, like a real coyote, deceitful, greedy, and ungrateful, but he could also help the Wishram people. Like all tricksters, he could bring both trouble and help to the world.

Alongside tricksters were transformers, who were usually guardian spirits of people. Many tribes thought that the great animal spirits, like the tricksters and transformers, were responsible for creating humans.

Linking the Native Americans with the spirit world were the shamans. The shaman was both a medicine man (a healer) and a religious leader. He or she was considered to be in close contact with the spirit world of the ancestors and with the spirits of the natural world, such as the spirits of the corn (maize), the sun, and thunder.

Although Native Americans believed in an afterlife, ideas of the spirit world, or exactly what happened to one's spirit after death, varied. The shaman was responsible for guiding spirits to the "right" place and for making sure that the living people conducted the appropriate rituals properly.

THE VISION QUEST

Plains tribes, especially the Cheyenne and the Sioux, believed one way of contacting the spirits and receiving their guidance was through the ritual known as the vision quest. It was the shaman's responsibility to help young tribe members succeed at this rite.

A vision quest could occur several times during a person's lifetime, but traditionally it was felt important for teenage boys — and some girls — to experience the ritual.

Vision quests varied, but some aspects of the following description generally applied. To begin, the youth might gather several specific items, as instructed by the shaman. These ranged from certain types of grass and herbs to feathers and animal skins.

Above: *A Plains warrior's shield with the design of a bear facing a hail of bullets. The design was meant to give the warrior protection in battle.*

Below: *Chief Mountain, in Montana, was sacred to the Blackfoot tribe. Worshipers would travel to the mountain for spiritual growth.*

Once collected the items would be blessed and specially prepared by the shaman. Next the shaman and the youth smoked tobacco together as an offering to the spirits that they wanted to contact.

Then the youth would cleanse his body, inside and out. This included sweating in a sweat lodge, much like a sauna, and drinking an herbal concoction. The drink caused vomiting, therefore purifying the youth's insides. During this part and the final phase of the ritual the youth would pray out loud for the strength to withstand the power of the spirit world.

Finally, the youth journeyed far away from his camp to find a place to fast for several days. At the secluded spot he would wait for the appearance of a spirit guide who would teach him how to live. The spirit would also give him a secret song or tell him a secret way to paint his face as a means of contacting the spirit world.

The Father of Corn

No other crop was as important to Native Americans as corn, which is durable and easy to grow. This Ojibwa myth provides a divine explanation for the crop's origin.

A POOR FAMILY LIVED A LONG TIME ago in the cold land of the Great Lakes. The father of the family was a good man who was grateful to the Great Spirit for everything nature provided. But the father was a bad hunter, and often the family was hungry.

The eldest son, Wunzh, had inherited his father's gentle nature. When he was old enough for the ritual to find the spirit that would guide him through life, he went off to a secluded hut where he had to fast for seven days. He spent the first couple of days admiring the beauty of nature, wondering why some plants were so good to eat when others were poisonous.

On the third day, as he lay on his bed, weak from not eating, he saw a young man float down from the sky. The stranger was dressed in a beautiful costume of green and yellow with a plume of waving feathers on his head. The stranger told Wunzh that the Great Spirit had sent him to show Wunzh how to help his tribe survive without hunting and fishing.

The stranger commanded Wunzh to get out of bed and wrestle with him. Although Wunzh felt weak, he wanted to show the stranger that he was brave. He fought until he could fight no more. The stranger said he would return the next day to continue the challenge. After the second time this happened the stranger said he would return once more for a final test.

Strangely, as Wunzh's body had grown weaker each day, his mind had grown stronger. On the seventh day he fought the stranger again, but this time Wunzh won. The stranger took off his beautiful clothes and ordered Wunzh to dig a hole. The stranger climbed into the hole, gave Wunzh a list of instructions — they made no sense to the young man — and ordered Wunzh to bury him.

As the stranger had ordered, Wunzh returned often to water and weed the patch. Through the spring he visited the site, and at the end of summer he took his father to see it. A large corn plant with bright silken hair and nodding plumes of green leaves was waving in the breeze. Wunzh told his father about the stranger, the challenges, and the instructions on how to grow and harvest corn. He also explained how the corn should be cooked close to the fire until the golden husk had become brown. When the family ate their first meal of corn, they praised the Great Spirit for his gift.

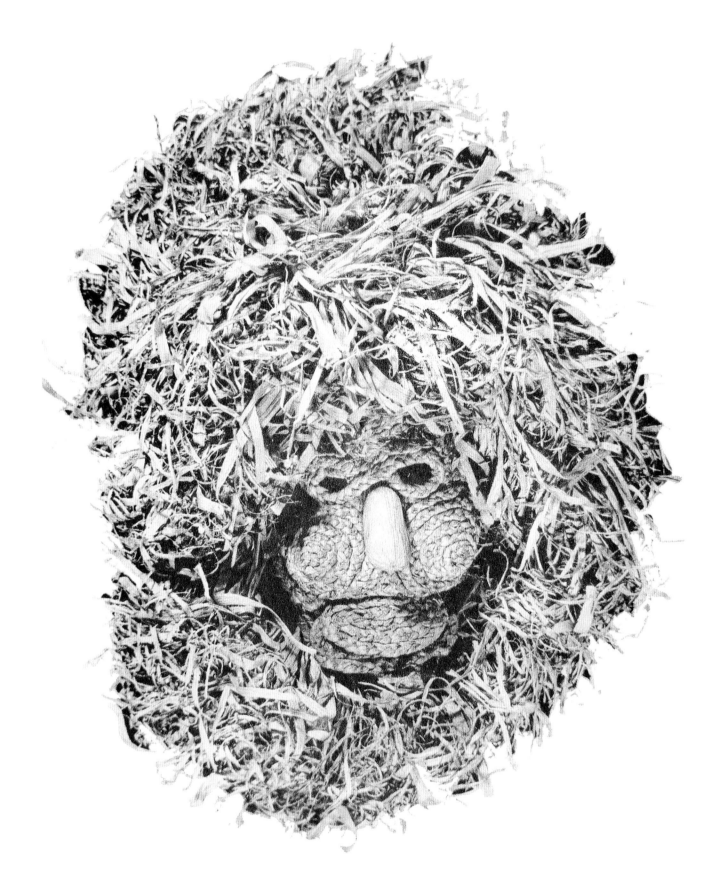

Above: *This Iroquoian corn mask was worn at special ceremonies held to celebrate the importance of corn in the tribe's daily life. Tribes across North America held similar rituals, usually during planting season or at harvest time.*

The Importance of Corn and Farming

As the first settlers discovered, Native Americans were expert farmers. Indeed, even in parts of the buffalo-dominated Plains, there were tribes that farmed as well as hunted.

Corn was the most important crop for Native Americans. Besides being a crop that could be stored year round, corn stalks were woven into thatch for housing, and the husks were made into twined blankets. The Ojibwa and other tribes told many stories about corn and performed rituals and dances especially for the planting and harvest seasons.

Corn was originally farmed by Mesoamerican tribes thousands of years ago, and by the time Christopher Columbus first set foot in North America in 1492, the crop was being grown by tribes across the whole continent. Planting corn was easy. All it took was forming a small mound of earth, making a deep hole in the mound using a stick, and then dropping four or five kernels of corn into the hole.

By the 16th century many tribes were planting corn alongside other crops such as pumpkins, peppers, gourds, beans, and squashes, which

reduced the growth of weeds near the corn and gave villages a varied and reliable supply of vegetables.

Corn, one of the most versatile crops, could be grown in all regions except in the cold Subarctic and Arctic. In the desert conditions of the Southwest, where average annual rainfall measured as little as 13 inches (33 cm), the ancient Hohokam tribe,

Above: Two holy spirits flank the sacred corn plant on this Navajo blanket. The Navajo, like so many tribes, believed that corn was a gift from the spirit world.

which existed from around 300 B.C. until the mid-1400s, engineered an irrigation network that included wide, shallow trenches with dams and valves made of woven mat that controlled the flow of precious water onto the fields. In addition many Native American tribes in the region performed special rituals and dances meant to cause enough rainfall to nourish the crops.

FARMS AND VILLAGES

The development of farming in North America, beginning some 5,500 years ago, caused a drastic change in the lifestyle of the early Native Americans. For centuries leading up to this period early Native Americans were mostly hunter-gatherers without a permanent home, always having to be on the move in search of food, whether wild game, berries, or nuts. With farming,

Above: *This 16th-century painting of an East Coast Native American village includes a corn field (center right).*

Below: *The artist George Catlin, while traveling through Native American villages, made this painting in the early 1830s after witnessing a Native American Green Corn fertility dance.*

however, communities could settle in one fertile place, build villages, and grow most, if not all, their own food.

Nevertheless, there were some communities, referred to by modern historians as Plains-village tribes, who lived part of the year in a permanent village and the rest of the time following buffalo herds. These tribes would plant their crops in the spring, leave the village to hunt buffalo in the summer, and return to the village in the late fall in time to harvest the crops.

Wisagatcak and the Creation

This Cree myth, which explains how land was created, contains many elements that would have been familiar to Native Americans in the Subarctic, including beaver dams and springs.

ONE DAY, WISAGATCAK built a dam out of stakes that he placed across a creek. He wanted to trap the Great Beaver when he swam out of his lodge. Wisagatcak waited all day and was getting very bored when finally, as dusk fell, he spotted the Great Beaver swimming toward him and the dam. He took hold of his spear, aimed it at the Great Beaver, but just as he got ready to throw it a muskrat bit him in the bottom, causing him to miss. Angry and frustrated, Wisagatcak gave up hunting the Great Beaver for the night.

The next morning he decided to break the dam apart, so he took down all the stakes. Water began flowing out, but Wisagatcak could not believe his eyes. The water level was rising instead of falling. He tried desperately to stop the water flowing everywhere, but the Great Beaver had used his magic powers and cast a spell on the water. Soon the whole world was covered with water.

Having raced to the top of a nearby mountain, Wisagatcak pulled up hundreds of trees to make a large raft before the water got too deep. Then he helped as many different animals on board as

the large raft could carry. These included the muskrat, the raven, the wolf, and many others.

After two relentless weeks the Great Beaver finally stopped making the water rise. The muskrat volunteered to be the first to leave the raft in search of dry land. He swam for many hours until he grew tired and drowned. Then the raven left the raft. He flew for a whole day looking for land, but all he could see in every direction was water.

The next day Wisagatcak decided to use his own magic and asked the wolf to help him. He made the wolf run along the edge of the raft with a ball of moss in his mouth. As he ran the moss grew larger and larger until dry land started to form on it. Then the wolf put the land down and the animals danced around it, singing powerful spells as they circled it.

The land grew wider and wider in every direction, spreading across the large raft and eventually covering most of the world. Some water remained underneath the earth, however. Today when water springs up through holes in the ground, it is because of cracks appearing in Wisagatcak's large raft.

Above: *Throughout the Eastern Woodlands and Subarctic regions springs, like cracks in Wisagatcak's raft, feed streams, creeks, rivers, ponds, and lakes that were essential to Native American life.*

The Importance of Water in the Subarctic

Tribes who lived in the Subarctic region relied on lakes and rivers to supply them with fish for food, small game for clothing, and a method of travel.

Below: *Thousands of lakes, streams, and rivers dot the Subarctic region, which can help create misty atmospheric scenes.*

Water was central to the lives of the Cree and the other Subarctic tribes. They depended on lakes and rivers for sources of food and transportation and thought that all nature contained powerful spirits such as Wisagatcak and the Great Beaver.

The Subarctic region covers most of Canada's Northwest Territories and the provinces from Manitoba in the west to Newfoundland in the east, and the edge of the Arctic tundra in the north to the Great Lakes in the south. The landscape is made up of thick pine forests interspersed with thousands of rivers and lakes. All the waterways and land freeze over during winter, which in the extreme north lasts six months, and thaw out during the short summer.

In the early 19th century, when European explorers first made contact with the Cree, their hunting territory stretched from the Ottawa River in the east to the Saskatchewan River in the

Left: *A modern Cree fisherman catches fish in the traditional way by dropping a net through a hole atop a frozen lake.*

In the winter Cree hunters would get around on foot by wearing snowshoes to cross the flat, open expanses of the frozen lakes, rivers, and streams.

Once spring arrived, the land turned boggy as the snow melted and the forests became difficult to cross. For traveling, the tribes of the Subarctic and Eastern Woodlands used canoes to navigate the many rivers and lakes. The canoes were made out of strips of bark from birch or elm trees fixed over a framework of cedar splints. The joints between the bark strips were usually sewn together with pine roots and made watertight by sealing with pitch.

Below: *In the Subarctic, traveling by canoe was common, except during winter.*

The bark canoes were practical modes of transportation because they were lightweight and could glide quickly across the water. They were also light enough to carry across land.

west, a distance of some 1,200 miles (1,920 km). In this vast area Native Americans hunted moose, caribou, and smaller game such as hare and beaver and when possible gathered roots and berries. Farming was difficult because of the harsh winter conditions, but Native Americans thrived because they adapted their technology to suit the climate.

Fish such as salmon, char, pike, and trout also formed an important part of their diet. During the long winter months the Cree would camp near a frozen lake and fish through holes in the ice. This gave them an ample supply of food until spring arrived, when they could start hunting again.

ADJUSTING TO SEASONS

In summer the Cree moved their camps in search of animals to hunt. They lived in cone-shaped tents, similar to tepees, that were covered with birchbark. These birchbark tents were lightweight and easy to transport.

Raven Steals the Daylight

The Tsimshian tribe, along with others of the Pacific Northwest Coast region, believed that Raven, one of their most important deities, gave daylight to the world.

LONG AGO, BEFORE there was daylight and when the world was covered in darkness, Raven left the heavens and flew across the water for a very long time. As he grew tired he dropped a small stone his father had given him. The stone fell into the sea and turned into a large rock. Then Raven flew east until he reached the mainland. There he scattered salmon and trout roe (eggs) in the rivers so that they would be full of fish. He also dropped seeds onto the land to make plenty of fruit and berries for people.

One night clouds blocked the little light that the stars gave off, and Raven realized how hard it must be for people to look for food in total darkness. To help them he flew high up into the sky to the house of the Heaven Chief.

He had not been there long when the Heaven Chief's daughter came out with a bucket to fetch water. On seeing her, Raven turned himself into a leaf and dropped into her bucket. Without noticing the leaf, the Heaven Chief's daughter took a drink from the bucket and swallowed it. Immediately she became pregnant. The Heaven Chief and his wife were delighted soon afterward when she gave birth to a strong baby boy.

As the baby boy grew he kept crying and nothing would console him. The Heaven Chief summoned all the wise men of the heavens to ask their advice. One of them said that the baby wanted *mã*. The *mã* was the box in which daylight was kept, and it hung in a corner of the Heaven Chief's house.

The Heaven Chief gave the baby the box, and as soon as he took it he stopped crying. For the next four days he played with it all the time until the Heaven Chief stopped noticing the baby's games. Then he started to cry again, and the Heaven Chief felt sorry for him. He told his daughter to find out what the problem was. She listened to the baby and understood that he wanted to look at the sky but could not see it because the smoke hole in the ceiling of the house was sealed.

To make the baby happy, the Heaven Chief opened the smoke hole. At once the baby changed back into Raven. Grasping the box containing the daylight, he flew out of the smoke hole and back down to the earth. Raven landed on top of a mountain. Taking the light out of the box, he threw it everywhere, bringing daylight to people.

Above: *The myth of Raven and the box of daylight is depicted in this Northwest Coast ceremonial hat from the middle of the 19th century. The hat is made from many different materials, including bird feathers and shells.*

The Rich Lives of the Northwest Coast Tribes

The Tsimshian, Nootka, Chinook, and other tribes who lived in the Northwest Coast region had many cultural similarities, such as the potlatch ceremony, and were expert traders.

The Tsimshian myth (see page 30) of Raven bringing abundance and daylight to people reflected the rich variety of food available to the tribes of the Pacific Northwest Coast. This region, stretching in a narrow band from Yakutat Bay in the Gulf of Alaska to Cape Mendocino in California, offered the greatest quantity and types of food in the whole of North America. The vast array included marine animals, large land mammals such as bear, moose, and elk, and numerous kinds of nuts and berries. But for many tribes fish was the main food source, and the fishermen developed a range of methods for catching fish, including trapping, netting, hooking, and spearing.

Left: *In the Pacific Northwest Coast region, large plank houses, such as the one shown here, often housed several different but related families of a tribe.*

Left: *One legend has it that Raven created the Queen Charlotte Islands (shown here), which are part of the Canadian province of British Columbia, in order to have a place to rest.*

Northwest Coast tribes lived in villages and were skilled carpenters best known for carving totem poles. There are several different kinds of totem poles, ranging from memorial ones, which were erected when a house changed owners, to ridicule poles, on which the likeness of an important person who had failed in some way was carved upside down. They could also be like family crests, where an image on the pole represented an important ancestor of the owner.

The Northwest Coast tribes built large houses out of giant cedar trees that they felled and split into planks. In some villages, the whole village might live in the same plank house. The biggest house is thought to have been 650 feet long by 60 feet wide (196 m by 18 m). In the center was a fire pit used for heating the house and cooking. The houses were open, although if a family wanted more privacy they could use a moveable screen. Each family's possessions were stored in the house.

Potlatch Ceremony

The potlatch was both a religious and social ceremony held by many Northwest Coast tribes. It was used to celebrate a range of events, including a new house, erecting a totem pole, or a marriage. The heart of the ceremony was the giving of gifts by the host. This was not done to be generous but to place the receiver of the gift under obligation to the host.

Following a potlatch, guests were expected to hold a bigger, more lavish potlatch in return. Often this brought either financial ruin or, if they refused to hold their own potlatch, shame.

There was also a spiritual aspect. The food eaten at a potlatch symbolized links to the spirit world. Eating a lot of salmon, for example, was a show of respect to the divine spirit of fish.

Sedna, Goddess of the Sea

The Inuit depended on fish and sea mammals for survival. They believed that the temperamental goddess Sedna decided whether hunters would have a good catch or not.

SEDNA, AN INUIT GIRL, lived alone with her father. She was very beautiful and many men wanted to marry her. But Sedna was as vain as she was beautiful and refused them all.

One day a man arrived in the village who was more handsome than any of her other admirers. His kayak was decorated with jewels, and he wore the finest furs and carried a spear made out of solid ivory. From his canoe he called to Sedna, "Be my wife and come away with me." He promised her that she would never be hungry or need to work if she married him. Sedna was so impressed that she packed her bags and left with the stranger without telling her father.

For two days they sailed, and during the journey Sedna noticed that her new husband began to change. First his jewels and spear disappeared, then his skin fell away to reveal feathers. His eyes grew beady and feathers covered his face.

When they arrived at his home his true identity was revealed. He was a bird-spirit. His house was a nest and the meat he brought her was only freshly killed gulls. It was true Sedna did not have to work, but she hated living in the nest and cried when she thought of her father.

Meanwhile, her father was lonely and decided to find Sedna. After sailing for many days he found her sitting alone in the nest. The bird-spirit was away hunting. Sedna explained what had happened and together they sailed away.

When the bird-spirit returned to the empty nest, he vowed to reclaim his wife. Flying above the icy sea, it did not take him long to catch up to the boat. Swooping down, he tried to seize Sedna, but her father severely injured him with an oar. Realizing he was beaten the bird-spirit flew away, but as he disappeared a fierce storm blew up. Huge waves crashed against the boat, and the father was unable to steer it. Sedna screamed at her father to do something, but he was powerless.

"The sea is angry because you left your husband," her father shouted. A mad look came over his face, and he threw Sedna overboard. She clung on to the edge of the boat, but her father struck her right hand with his ax, cutting off her fingers. The severed fingers fell into the sea and became seals. Then he hit her left hand and those fingers became whales. Finally, Sedna herself disappeared under the water, transforming into the goddess of the sea and ending the storm.

Above: *Off Frederick Sound in Alaska, whales often breach — leap out of the water — as they migrate to the Arctic. The Inuit believed that Sedna, the goddess of the sea, was the source of the first whales.*

The Inuit and the Sea

The cold, harsh conditions of the Arctic made life hard for Inuit who lived in the frozen region. Survival often meant taking life-threatening risks, like hunting whales.

The Inuit believed that Sedna, as the goddess of the sea, provided them with most of their food. To keep Sedna happy, so the tradition goes, the Inuit had to hold certain ceremonies performed by the whole community. These ceremonies varied from community to community and place to place. But in all cases it was believed that angering Sedna might prompt her to stop providing sea mammals for the Inuit to hunt and eat.

Well into the 20th century the Inuit lived in much the same way as their ancestors did 5,000 years ago, when they first crossed the Bering Strait. They depended on the sea for survival and inhabited coastal areas that spread across some 7.5 million square miles (20 million sq. km), from Siberia, across northern Canada, to Greenland.

In addition to forming the main part of their diet, whales, seals, and walruses also gave the premodern Inuit material for clothing, weapons, fuel, making summer tents, and many other things.

In the long arctic winter, which lasts from September to May, the Inuit mainly hunted seals. When the sea freezes over, seals make breathing holes in the ice. The hunters would wait by these breathing holes to catch them when they came up for air.

In summer, when the ice starts to melt, seals and other sea mammals like walruses are easier to catch because they climb out of the water to sun themselves on the melting ice floes. Inuit hunters crawled up silently behind the mammals on the ice floes and harpooned them.

One of the most dangerous parts of Inuit life was whale hunting. Using umiaks — open wooden boats that usually sat 10 people — the hunters sailed among a small group, or pod, of whales so that the harpooner could get

Above: *This Inuit mask of a seal blowing bubbles was carved from wood in the early 20th century and may have been worn by children.*

Left: *A pair of Inuit hunters, photographed in 1928, having killed a seal. The dead mammal would have provided much needed food and perhaps clothing for the hunters' village.*

Below: *For shelter the Inuit made the best use of their frozen environment by carving ice blocks to build igloos. This modern Inuit igloo was built in Greenland.*

close enough to spear one. Once the whale was injured the hunters harpooned it several more times until it finally died. The risk of being capsized while hunting such huge mammals was worth taking because just one large whale could provide tons of meat for a whole community.

EATERS OF RAW MEAT

Because of the arctic climate the Inuit lacked fruits and vegetables, foods that prevent scurvy (a disease caused by the lack of vitamin C). But the Inuit were able to obtain the necessary vitamins by eating fresh meat, sometimes raw; cooking and processing meat removes some of the vitamins.

Algonquin-speaking Subarctic tribes called the Inuit "Eskimos," which means eaters of dogs or raw meat. Although the name was probably meant as an insult, white settlers used it more often than "Inuit," and it remains common.

The Girl in the Sky

On the Great Plains the sky dominates the flat landscape. This Arapaho myth shows the Plains tribe's fascination with both the sky and nature.

ONE DAY THE YOUNG SAPANA was gathering firewood. At the bottom of a giant cottonwood tree she saw a porcupine. She wanted its quills for her embroidery, so she tried to catch it. The animal raced up the tree and Sapana followed.

The tree seemed to go all the way to the sky. When she got to the top, Sapana saw what looked like a shining wall above her. It was the sky. Suddenly she found herself in the middle of a floating camp in the clouds, and the porcupine had turned into an ugly old man.

The old man took Sapana to his family's tepee. Once inside he put her right to work, scraping buffalo hides and making robes.

Every morning the old man went hunting, leaving Sapana to dig wild turnips. He warned her not to dig too deep, but one day she pulled up a very large turnip that left a hole in the cloud. Down below she saw her village. Carefully replacing the turnip over the hole, Sapana thought up a way to escape.

She began by secretly collecting strips of sinew left over from buffalo hides that she tied together to make a long rope. Then, while the old man was out hunting, she laid her digging stick across the hole. She tied one end of the rope to the stick and the other around her waist and lowered herself through the hole.

Although the rope was long, the floating camp was much higher than Sapana had realized. When she reached the end of the rope she was still far from the ground. She hung on swinging in the air, not sure what to do. Then the rope began to shake violently. The old man was pulling at the rope and throwing stones down on her.

Close by a buzzard circled. Sapana asked him for help. She climbed on the buzzard's back, and he started to descend. But Sapana was too heavy. The buzzard called to a hawk, who took her on his back. Soon the hawk too grew tired and she got back onto the buzzard. Finally he dropped her at her village, and before she could thank the birds, they both flew away.

When Sapana's parents saw her they were very happy. She told everyone about her adventure and the kindness of the buzzard and the hawk. From then on, as a show of thanks to the birds, her tribe always left one animal for the buzzard and hawk to eat after a hunt.

Above: *Giant cumulonimbus clouds — perhaps the type of cloud from which Sapana escaped — appear like floating mountains in the sky, forming dramatic contrasts to the gently rolling landscape of the Great Plains.*

Watching the Vast Sky over the Great Plains

With its vast, empty spaces and endless horizons, the Great Plains is a landscape dominated by the sky. The mythology and art of the Plains peoples reflects this inescapable fact.

On the Great Plains — an area between the Rocky Mountains and the Mississippi River that stretches from Texas in the south to Alberta, Canada, in the north — the landscape is almost flat and the horizon can appear miles away. For the Native Americans who roamed this vast region — including the Arapaho, Assiniboine, Blackfoot, Cheyenne, Comanche, Crow, Kiowa, and Sioux — with no valleys, forests, or hills to obstruct their view, everything was dominated by the sky. The importance both the day and night skies held for Plains tribes is reflected in the stories they told, in the many sky spirits they worshiped, and in the way they lived.

The sky spirits controlled everything from spectacular sunsets to violently dramatic thunderstorms, as well as all that happened on the ground. For many tribes the Sky Father, the most important heavenly spirit, was believed to exist in everything and everywhere,

much like the Christian God, protecting the tribespeople and, along with the other sky spirits, guiding the animals. Together the powers of all the heavenly spirits extended to altering the paths of migrating buffalo and causing rivers to dry up.

The Plains tribespeople believed that severe weather, such as lightning, thunderstorms, and hail, were signs of displeasure from the sky spirits. To

Above: *Although tepees were practical and portable shelters for Plains tribes, they provided no safety during violent weather such as tornadoes.*

Left: *Travois, A-shaped frames with a closed end that fitted over a horse, were used to transport frail people, goods, and tepees across the Great Plains. They were easy to assemble.*

keep all the spirits happy the people performed ceremonies, including the Sun Dance (see pages 16–17). This was essential because the Plains, then as now, experience some of the most extreme weather found anywhere in North America.

The flat landscape and lack of large natural barriers left the Plains tribes wide open to the devastating effects of violent thunderstorms and tornadoes. For instance, a large tornado — with wind speeds reaching 300 miles per hour (450 kph) — can devastate anything in its path. An exposed tepee on the Plains would be instantly destroyed.

STAR GAZERS

The night sky also played an important role in the mythology and lives of Plains tribes. For example, the semi-nomadic Pawnee — who traveled part of the year in search of

Below: *On the right side of this shaman's model tepee are painted the sun, moon, and a star.*

buffalo but kept a permanent village where crops were grown — arranged their lodges in the shape of the constellations. Tepees, shields, and clothing of all Plains tribes were often decorated with stars and the moon.

In myth, the morning star (Venus) was thought of as a warrior who cleared the sky before the sun returned from the underworld at the start of each new day. In keeping with this idea, tepees in most tribal camps on the Great Plains were laid out so that the entrance flaps opened east toward the morning sun.

The four major geographical directions — north, south, east, and west — also held great fascination for Plains tribes. They saw north as the direction from which cold rains and blizzards came and therefore thought of it as the direction of starvation and disease. The four major directions also matched the life stages of every living thing, with birth being the east and old age the north.

The Coming of the Buffalo

No other animal is more closely associated with Native Americans than the buffalo. This Dakota myth illustrates the divine importance the tribe placed on the animal.

ONE DAY, TWO YOUNG MEN were hunting for buffalo on the Great Plains when they saw a lone figure coming toward them from the west. The figure was moving as fast as a buffalo but it did not look like one.

When the figure got close enough, the men saw that it was a beautiful woman dressed in a buckskin dress with leggings and moccasins. The left side of the woman's hair was tied with coarse buffalo hair and in her right hand she carried a fan of flat sage. She told the two men that she had been sent by the buffalo tribe and that they must go home and prepare a special tepee for her. She went on to explain that once they had finished it she would visit them, bringing an important gift for their whole tribe.

As the beautiful woman was giving her instructions one of the men had impure thoughts about her. Sensing his thoughts, the woman stared into the man's eyes, and immediately a cloud came down and covered him in mist. When the mist cleared, only the man's skeleton was left. The woman told the other man, frozen with fear, to return to his tribe without looking back and to heed what she had said.

Terrified, the hunter ran back to camp and told his elders about the beautiful woman. They followed her instructions exactly. Promptly at sunrise the morning after the tepee was finished the woman entered the camp, this time carrying a large pipe in both hands.

The chiefs greeted her warmly, thanked her for her visit, invited her into the special tepee, and told her she was welcome to share their food. But since they were poor and had caught no buffalo, all they had to offer was water. The maiden sipped the water, then spoke to the chiefs. She told them that Wakan'tanka, chief of the buffalo tribe, looked kindly on them because of their goodness and honesty.

The pipe she had brought was a gift from Wakan'tanka and was to be used as a means of making peace with other nations. She praised the women of the tribe for working hard to keep the families together, and she talked to the children, telling them to respect their parents.

Then she turned to the men of the tribe and told them the pipe would help them, but only if they followed her rules. They must always obey the weather and the elements, otherwise nature

Above: *White buffalo, like the one the buffalo woman transforms into, are very rare. Native Americans of the Great Plains greatly respected such animals, believing them to be omens of a good future for the whole tribe.*

would take revenge on the tribe. Whenever they needed buffalo, they must smoke the pipe before a hunt. Then they would find plenty to kill.

She lit the pipe and pointed it to the sky in a show of respect to Wakan'tanka, then she pointed it to the ground, from where came gifts such as corn. The woman then took a puff from the pipe, passed it to the chiefs, and got up to leave. As she left the tepee she transformed into a white buffalo calf and disappeared.

A Native American Life Style Based on the Buffalo

In the summer, when buffalo herds stormed across the Great Plains in their thousands, many tribes followed, hunting for the food, clothing, and other things the animal provided.

According to the Dakota Sioux myth (see page 42), the beautiful woman who turned into a white buffalo promised the tribe that if they followed certain rules they would always have enough buffalo to eat. This myth reflected how important buffalo (*Bison bison*) was to the tribe's culture. In fact, buffalo was key to the survival of all Plains tribes, not just as food but also for clothing, weapons, and shelter.

For thousands of years, long before the arrival of the horse on the Plains in the mid-17th and early 18th centuries, buffalo were hunted on foot. This was dangerous, because buffalo are fast, strong, and fearsome creatures. Weighing as much as 2,000 lb (1,000 kg), a buffalo could easily trample a person to death. Until the 19th century buffalo herds were extremely large, with a single herd numbering in the thousands.

To hunt buffalo, Plains tribesmen had to be cunning and brave. Buffalo have poor eyesight, so some hunters in

Right: *The buffalo was nearly extinct 100 years ago, but due to decades of careful husbandry several herds are now thriving.*

mountainous areas of the West would trick herds into stampeding over a cliff.

But on the Plains, where there were few natural features like cliffs, hunting the animals was difficult, since they could run away easily. It became easier, however, with the arrival of the horse to the region.

Above: Hunting buffalo on horseback greatly increased the number of buffalo killed by Native Americans.

The horse not only allowed the Plains tribes to hunt buffalo more efficiently, it also brought numerous other tribes to the region who learned to hunt the animals on horseback.

Summer was the season for buffalo hunting. But every year the Plains tribes worried about whether they would catch enough buffalo to last the tribe until the next summer. To try to guarantee a successful hunt, the tribes held rituals to encourage the return of the herds. During the buffalo hunt Sioux leaders carried two insignia considered crucial for a good hunt — a feathered staff and a buffalo pipe, like the one given to the chiefs by the beautiful buffalo woman in the myth.

Using the Buffalo

A dead buffalo offered far more than just cooked and dried meat to the Plains tribes. Warm robes, tepees, and bedding could be made from buffalo hide. Bones could be turned into hand tools, and buffalo hoofs could be boiled down to make a kind of glue. Shields were shaped from the thick skin of a buffalo's neck, and a buffalo's stomach was made into a leak-proof bag for carrying water. The tail could be made into a fly whisk, and the sinews dried and stretched to form strong ropes and cords. Even buffalo dung was discovered to be useful, as a hot, slow-burning fuel.

Right: Stretching and tanning buffalo hide, as shown here, strengthens it for use as clothing and shelter, among other things.

Glossary

Algonquian The most common Native American language, it originated some 10,000 years ago in the **Eastern Woodlands** region and spread to the northern Great Plains.

Athapascan Native American language group of western North America. Speakers include some tribes in Canada and the Apache and Navajo in the **Southwest**.

beautiful buffalo woman In Dakota Sioux mythology, she gave a large pipe to the tribe to smoke when in need of buffalo.

Caddoan Native American language that originated in the **Southeast** but is spoken by tribes who formerly lived west of the Mississippi River such as the Caddo, Pawnee, and Wichita.

Coyote In Wishram mythology, an animal spirit who, with the help of Eagle, killed **Frog** and tried to steal the spirits of those who had died.

Eastern Woodlands Region that extends from the northern evergreen forests and the Great Lakes and Atlantic areas of Canada and the U.S. south to the Ohio Valley and west to the Mississippi. Tribes of the region generally included those who spoke either **Algonquian**, **Siouan**, or **Iroquoian**.

Frog In Wishram mythology, he was the master of the lodge where the spirits of the dead dwelled.

Great Beaver In Cree mythology an animal spirit who caused the old world to flood.

Great Chief In the Iroquoian myth "The Dueling Brothers," he was a

mighty sky spirit who banished his wife from their cloud home when he discovered she was pregnant.

Great Chief's wife In the Iroquoian myth "The Dueling Brothers," she was the grandmother of **Tsenta** and Taweskare.

Great Plains Vast flat region east of the Rockies that stretches from Texas to Alberta, Canada. It was where the buffalo roamed.

Great Spirit The force behind or present throughout creation; believed in by most tribes, although referred to by different names.

Great Turtle In the Iroquoian myth "The Dueling Brothers," he was leader of the animals on earth.

Heaven Chief In Tsimshian mythology, the keeper of daylight whose daughter is tricked into giving birth to **Raven**.

Iroquoian One of the two major Native American languages in the **Eastern Woodlands** region. In addition to the tribes of the **Iroquois Confederacy**, other speakers include the Cherokee.

Iroquois Confederacy League of **Eastern Woodlands** tribes made up of the Mohawk, Oneida, Onondaga, Cayuga, Seneca, and Tuscarora.

mã Tsimshian mythological box in which daylight was kept. It was stolen from the **Heaven Chief** by **Raven** and given to humans.

Mockingbird Hopi spirit who assigned the "ancient people" to different tribes and languages as they escaped the underworld.

Muskogean The dominant Native American tongue of the **Southeast**, spoken by the Chickasaw, Choctaw, Creek, and Seminole.

Northwest Coast Densely forested and mountainous region that stretches thinly southward from the Gulf of Alaska to northern California, and includes tribes such as the Chinook, Coast Salish, Haida, Kwakiutl, Nootka, Tlingit, and Tsimshian.

Old Man Coyote In Crow mythology, he created, among other creatures, humans and gave them fire and weapons to use when hunting.

potlatch Ceremony practiced by many **Northwest Coast** tribes that involved a host throwing a large feast and giving gifts to the guests.

Raven In Tsimshian mythology, a hero spirit who steals daylight from the **Heaven Chief** for humans.

Sapana In Arapaho mythology, she escaped the cloud home of an ugly old spirit and was rescued by a buzzard and a hawk.

Sedna Inuit goddess of the sea.

semi-nomadic A word describing people who travel for part of the year to find food.

Sequoya Born around 1760 and died in 1843, he was the creator of the Cherokee alphabet.

shaman Important member of a tribe who led rituals and was able to call on the spirit world to, among other things, heal the sick.

Siouan A Native American language spoken by the Assiniboine,

Crow, Iowa, Osage, and the Dakota, Nakota, and Lakota Sioux, among others. The area that the language formerly covered ranged from the Great Lakes to Texas.

Southeast A vast region spreading from the Mississippi River to Florida and the Gulf of Mexico to Virginia, and included tribes such as the Cherokee, Chickasaw, Choctaw, Creek, and Seminole.

Southwest A region covering roughly southern Utah and Colorado, Arizona, New Mexico, west Texas, and northern Mexico, and included tribes such as the Apache, Hopi, Navajo, and Pueblo.

Spider Woman Hopi spirit who with **Mockingbird** helped the "ancient people" escape the underworld when it was flooding.

Sun Dance Ceremonial dance performed annually by several Plains tribes in order to renew their spiritual beliefs.

transformers Mythological characters who were usually guardians of people.

tricksters Complicated mythological characters who could be both troublemakers and heroes.

Tsenta The mythological father of the Iroquois and grandson of **Great Chief's wife**. His younger brother was the angry Taweskare, who made the snakes poisonous.

umiak wooden open boats used by Inuit fishermen.

Uto-Aztecan A Native American language spoken by various tribes of

the **Southwest**, including the Comanche, Hopi, and Pueblo.

vision quest Grueling ritual, usually performed by a young person, intended to introduce a lifelong guide from the spirit world.

Wakan'tanka In Sioux mythology, the spirit chief of the buffalo.

White People A mythological group of ancient Hopi who were the first to see the sun.

Wisagatcak In Cree mythology, he created the current world from atop a giant raft after the old world was flooded by the **Great Beaver**.

Wunzh In Ojibwa mythology, a young tribesman who was given divine instructions on how to cultivate corn.

Further Reading & Viewing

BOOKS

Bial, Raymond. *Lifeways: The Apache.* Tarrytown, NY: Benchmark Books, 2000.

Clare, John D. *American Indian Life.* Hauppauge, NY: Barrons Juveniles, 2000.

Copeland, Peter F. *Great Native Americans.* Mineola, NY: Dover Publications, 1997.

Hook, Jason, and Richard Hook. *People Who Make History: Native Americans.* Austin, TX: Raintree/ Steck Vaughn, 2001.

Wood, Marion. *Myths and Civilizations of the Native Americans.* New York, NY: Peter Bedrick Books, 1998.

Yoe, Charlotte, and David Yoe. *The Wigwam and the Longhouse.* Boston, MA: Houghton Mifflin, 2000.

VIDEOS

Native Americans: The Nations of the Northeast. Turner Home Entertainment, 1994.

Native Americans: The People of the Great Plains, Part 1. Turner Home Entertainment, 1994.

Native Americans: Tribes of the Southeast. Turner Home Entertainment, 1994.

WEBSITES

Encyclopedia Mythica: An Encyclopedia on Mythology, Folklore, and Legend. http://www.pantheon.org/mythica

Mythology of North American Indians. http://www. windows.umich.edu

Native American History Archive: A New Center for Native American Studies in International Classrooms. http:// www.ilt.columbia.edu/k12/naha

Index